Littlenose

More adventures of

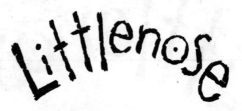

Littlenose the Hero
Littlenose the Hunter
Littlenose the Joker

Littlenose
the Explorer

JOHN GRANT
Illustrations by Ross Collins

SIMON AND SCHUSTER

SIMON AND SCHUSTER
The Ice Monster was first published in 1972
The Giant Snowball was first published in 1972
Urk was first published in 1976
Littlenose's Hibernation was first published in 1982
Ice was first published in 1983
in Great Britain by The British Broadcasting Corporation

This collection published by Simon & Schuster UK Ltd, 2007
A CBS COMPANY

1 3 5 7 9 10 8 6 4 2

Simon & Schuster UK Ltd
Africa House
64-78 Kingsway
London WC2B 6AH

A CIP catalogue record for this book is available from the British Library

ISBN 9781416926689

Typeset by Ana Molina
Printed and bound in Great Britain by Cox & Wyman Ltd, Reading, Berkshire

Contents

Littlenose's Hibernation

It had been snowing all night; come to think of it, it had been snowing all *week*. The Ice Age landscape was covered in snow . . . and ice, of course. In the caves of the Neanderthal folk, snores came from under fur bedclothes, while the sun rose reluctantly over the trees, its pale winter light shining into the caves to tell people that it was time to get up.

Littlenose poked his berry-sized nose out of the covers, and quickly pulled it back again. He screwed up his eyes and shivered.

"If I had *my* way," he thought, "no one would get up at this time of year. Everyone would stay in bed until spring." He pulled the covers closer around his ears, but only succeeded in letting in a cold draught.

The cold draught was nothing to the icy blast which hit him as Dad dragged the covers off. "Up you get," he shouted. "You can't lie there all day. There's work to be done. We're out of firewood, and Mum needs water from the river before she can make breakfast."

Pulling on his winter furs, Littlenose left the cave and trudged through the snow towards the river, a clay pot on his shoulder

and a stone axe in his hand. "Fill that pot!
Chop that wood! That's all I ever hear
these days," he muttered to himself.

He muttered while he broke a hole in
the river ice with the axe and filled the pot
with water. He was still muttering as he
brought it back to the cave,
and he continued to
mutter as he
chopped a branch
from a dead tree
and dragged it
home. "Stop
muttering," said
Mum. "I think
you must have
got out of bed
on the wrong
side this morning."

"If I had my way," thought Littlenose to himself, "I wouldn't have got out of *any* side of the bed at all."

Over breakfast, he continued to think: "People are stupid. Birds and animals have more sense. The elk left months ago for warmer places to spend the winter; and the wild geese flew far away to the south where it is always summer."

The last course for breakfast was a few hazel nuts. Littlenose crouched close to the fire to eat them. "Squirrels eat nuts," he said to himself. "They collect them in the autumn and only get up to eat one or two, if they wake up feeling peckish. They sleep more or less all winter. I wish I could do the same."

Suddenly, he jumped up, scattering nuts all over the floor. Why *couldn't* he sleep all winter, hibernate like the squirrels and the bears and the dormice? But it was not something to be done on the spur of the moment. It required a lot of thought.

That night after supper, Dad sat with an air of great concentration, binding a new flint point on to his spear, and Mum was sewing. Littlenose hesitated for a moment, then spoke to Mum. "I'm going to hibernate," he said.

"Well, do it quietly, dear," said Mum, without looking up. "Don't disturb Dad. You know what he's like when he's busy."

Littlenose started to say something, but decided not to. He *had* tried to tell them about his intentions and it shouldn't come as too much of a shock.

The shock was Littlenose's next morning. When Dad as usual pulled the covers off him, Littlenose pulled them right back on again. "I'm hibernating," he said, eyes shuttight. Next moment, he was standing shivering outside the cave where Dad had yanked him by one ear. His winter furs landed at his feet, and Dad shouted, "Get dressed, and stop this nonsense! There's work to do."

As he did his morning water and firewood fetching, Littlenose muttered more than usual, but he had to admit to himself that he had handled the whole scheme very badly. The problem was that the cave wasn't his; it was Dad's. And Dad made the rules. Bears and other hibernators prepared special places to spend the winter. He would have to do the same.

As soon as Dad and Mum were busy, Littlenose slipped into his own special corner of the cave and gathered up his bedding, plus a few fur rugs that no one appeared to be actually using at that precise moment. Then, looking like a large, round, furry animal with no head and two legs, he left the cave and set off through the snow. A cave of his own was what he was looking for. Not too big. Just somewhere he could roll up in his furs and dream the winter away. It was more difficult

than he had imagined. Caves weren't that
easily come by, and they all appeared to
belong to someone already.

Littlenose was a long way from home
when he spied the dark opening of a cave
among a pile of boulders. About time, too,
he thought. Although it was winter, the
noonday sun was warm, particularly to
someone laden down with fur bed-clothes.

He looked carefully around; there were no signs of a fire or anything else that might suggest people. Cautiously, he entered. The cave seemed spacious and had a soft, sandy floor. Might as well give it a try. Littlenose spread out the furs, then lay down and rolled himself up in them. It was perfect. And it seemed such a pity after coming all this way to waste such a find. He would start his hibernation there and then.

Littlenose woke with a start. Was it spring already? He didn't feel as if he had slept for very long. Something hit him gently on the head. He put his hand up to feel. His hair felt wet, and something hit the back of his hand . . . a drop of water.

Littlenose jumped up. He could hear it now. A steady drip, drip! He looked up.

The sun must be melting the snow, and the cave had a leaking roof. No wonder nobody lived here. He gathered up his bedding before it got too wet, and hurried out into the open again.

Well, the day was young. Still plenty of time to find a suitable cave. And only a short distance away, partly screened by a clump of bare trees, was another opening in the side of a high bank.

This time, Littlenose was taking no chances. He left his fur covers outside and carefully examined the floor for puddles and damp patches, and peered as well as he was able, into the gloom above his head for any sign of a leak. It seemed perfect! The trees outside cut off most of the light from the very back of the cave, but Littlenose groped around and spread the fur rugs and bed covers into a comfortable bed. Then he rolled himself up and closed his eyes to await the coming of spring.

Littlenose woke slowly. He felt quite refreshed. Was it spring already? Well, there was one way to find out. He made to push back the bed-clothes . . . and had a horrible surprise. He couldn't *move*!

Something seemed to be holding his arms tight. He couldn't move his body, although his legs seemed to be free. What had happened? Was it magic? Had he

perhaps blundered into a Straightnose cave
and they had put a spell on him? He tried
again, and found that he could move one
hand and arm just a bit. He began to
investigate with his fingers. All he could
feel was the fur of the bedclothes. He
could recognise each piece by the feel.
There was the grey wolf skin with its long,
soft fur. And the short soft fur of the cover
made from many rabbit skins stitched
together. And the tiger skin rug. The red
fox. The bear skin. The . . .! Wait a minute!

HE DIDN'T HAVE ANY BEAR SKIN
COVERS!

Pulling his fingers away from the bear
skin, he twisted his head as far round as he
could, and in the dim light from the cave
entrance, found himself looking straight
into the face of a sleeping bear. A sleeping

bear with one huge, hairy arm around
Littlenose, cuddling him as it slept.
Littlenose's heart almost stopped beating
with fright. What had happened? Had the
bear come in after he had gone to sleep? Or
was it already asleep and hibernating when
Littlenose had made up his bed in the
semi-darkness? It didn't really matter. What
mattered was getting out before the bear
woke. It might wake hungry, and Littlenose
didn't fancy being a midnight snack for a

hibernating bear. He struggled gently to free himself, and the bear wrapped its arm even tighter around him than before until he could scarcely breathe.

What was he to do? Kick the bear? Perhaps biting the bear might make it let go? On the other hand that was more likely to wake it up – the last thing he wanted to do. Desperately, he racked his brains for something that might make the bear let go but not waken it.

Ah, but there was a way, and it might just work. With the hand which had felt the fur covers, Littlenose reached up under the bear's arm, and tickled it. The bear gave a sort of snort and moved slightly. Again Littlenose tickled, and this time the bear gave a kind of bear giggle in its sleep and wriggled its shoulders. "It's working," thought Littlenose. Again and again, he tickled the bear, and each time it relaxed its grip a little, and even had a bear-like smile on its face. One last tickle and the bear humped right over on its other side, and Littlenose moved just in time to avoid being squashed. He was free! Stealthily, he pulled the fur bedding away from beside the sleeping bear. One cover wouldn't come, and he saw that the bear had it in a bundle, cuddling it instead of Littlenose. He decided to leave it.

With his bundle in his arms, Littlenose tip-toed from the cave, then ran as fast as his legs would carry him, expecting any moment an angry roar from the cave. But the bear was sound asleep again and dreaming bear dreams.

After all the trouble he had had, anyone

except Littlenose would have given up the whole idea of hibernating and gone home. Littlenose was made of sterner stuff. As he walked back towards the caves he thought, "Ready-made caves seem to have ready-made problems. It would be better if I could make my own cave. What is a cave, anyway? Only a pile of rocks with a hole in the middle." Finding enough rocks might be difficult. But it didn't *need* to be rocks!

A short distance from the caves where the tribe lived, he stopped. The snow lay firm and level all around, and Littlenose began to roll a snowball. When it was about knee-high he rolled another, and another, until he was surrounded by large snowballs. He made a ring of snowballs about four paces across. Then he built another slightly smaller ring on top, and

another on top of that. He went on until he had used up all his snowballs and filled in the gaps with handfuls of snow. It looked like a big heap of snow, but Littlenose knew that it was hollow inside like a cave. It was a pity he had forgotten to make a door, but he managed to drag one of the bottom snowballs out, and there it was. A custom-built cave made of snow! He crawled inside with his bedding. It was quite dry. Why hadn't he thought of this before? At last, his own hibernating cave.

Now, while Littlenose had been busy with his snow cave, another member of the tribe was hard at work, too. It was Nosey, chief tracker because of his remarkably handsome and sensitive Neanderthal nose. Now he came snuffling along, bent almost double in his winter hunting robe, his famous nose sticking out from the hood and held a mere hairsbreadth from the ground. The afternoon sun was still quite warm, and Nosey mopped his brow with the back of his hand. "Must be out of training," he said to himself. "Not only warm, bit out of puff, even on the level. Must have a rest."

He straightened his back and looked around. Where was he? What happened? No wonder he was breathless . . . he had been climbing a hill! But there shouldn't *be* a hill here, not even a small round-topped one like this he was standing on. Bit slippery too, the warm sun was beginning to melt the snow. Nosey could feel the snow dissolving beneath his feet, but before he could ponder the mystery further the whole thing caved in.

Littlenose thought the sky had fallen as Nosey landed with a soggy thump right on top of him. They both struggled out of the slushy mess together.

"YOU!" shouted Nosey. "I might have known it was one of your tricks! Wait till I see your Dad, my lad." And he stalked off, trying to look dignified with the inside of his robe full of melting snow.

But Littlenose paid no attention to Nosey or his threat. A sudden thought had come to him. He knew why people didn't hibernate. They would miss the Sun Dance, the great Neanderthal Midwinter festival! And that would never do. He'd really had a very narrow escape.

Littlenose gathered up his fur bedding and set off for home, wondering what Mum would say when she saw everything sopping wet. And would she believe that one of her best fur rugs had been stolen by a black bear?

Ice

Neanderthal boys didn't go to school. But, that is not to say that they didn't have to learn. Just to manage to stay alive in those days meant having to learn all sorts of useful things, like hunting and making fires. Most Neanderthal boys were taught by their dads and one cold winter's day, Littlenose was just coming to the end of a particularly dreary lecture from Dad on

. . . Well, actually, Littlenose had lost the thread so early on that he couldn't have said *what* the lecture was about. Suddenly, he was aware, by the change in Dad's voice, that he was getting to the end.

"Well, that's it," said Dad with a self-satisfied look. He rather fancied himself as a lecturer.

"Oh . . . eh . . . yes," said Littlenose.

"We've a moment or two before lunch," went on Dad. "Time for a question or two. Fire away."

"Oh," said Littlenose again. He thought hard for a moment, then said, "Why is ice?"

"What?" said Dad.

"Why is ice?" said Littlenose again. "I've been wondering. There *is* an awful lot of it."

Dad looked at Littlenose. "That must be

the silliest question I've ever heard. Why is ice, indeed? This is the Ice Age! There would be no point in calling it that if there were no ice, would there?"

"But there's no ice in summer," persisted Littlenose," and we don't call that the No-ice Age."

Dad said, "Hmph!" and Mum called, "Lunch is ready". And that was the end of the lesson.

Littlenose thought about it all through the meal and for most of the rest of the day. He fell asleep thinking about it, and it was the first thing on his mind when he woke next morning. After breakfast, he walked down to the river. It was frozen solid at this time of year, and perhaps just looking at such a lot of ice might suggest an answer. Two-Eyes had followed

Littlenose. "What do you think, Two-Eyes?" said Littlenose. Two-Eyes just sniffed. He had a slight cold in the trunk. A mammoth version of a cold in the nose. Much the same, really, but longer.

A line of figures had appeared on the frozen river. It was a hunting party setting out for the opposite bank. Well, there was one good use for ice. People could walk across rivers on it. You could slide on ice, too, of course. That was fun. At least Littlenose thought so, but the grown-ups spent a lot of time throwing ashes and cinders from the fire on to it, particularly on the best and most slippery places. They had no imagination, decided Littlenose. He broke a piece from the tip of an icicle and put it in his mouth. It tasted of nothing. It wasn't even much use for eating.

While all these thoughts had been passing through his mind, he had been walking on the ice of the river and, when he looked back, he found that he was about half-way across.

It was at that point that Littlenose saw
the fish. Beneath his feet and below the ice
was a perch. He could see it quite clearly.
"It's come up to have a look at me through
the ice," said Littlenose to himself. He
crouched down to have a closer look but
the perch didn't swim away at the sudden
movement. It didn't move a fin. Even when
Littlenose stood up and stamped his foot.

Then he saw why. The perch wasn't in water at all. It was in the ice! Trapped and motionless. When the first frosts of winter came, instead of staying safely at the bottom of the river, the stupid creature must have strayed too close to the surface, and when the river froze . . . it was caught. It was all very interesting. Littlenose called to Two-Eyes, "You'll never guess what I've found. Come and see!"

And Two Eyes slid down the bank and came running across the ice. Too late Littlenose realised his mistake. "Go back! I didn't mean it!" he shouted in alarm. "GO BACK!"

At the sound of Littlenose's voice, Two-Eyes ran even faster. When he did get the message, it was too late. He tried to stop . . . and slid along the ice. Littlenose tried

to run out of the way, but had taken half a
dozen steps when Two-Eyes knocked him
off his feet, and the went down together in
a heap with a solid thump on the ice. And
the ice broke. Not suddenly. It simply
cracked all around them, water spurting up
through. Then they fell in!

It wasn't particularly deep, but it was wet

and *very* cold. Two-Eyes trumpeted and Littlenose yelled as they scrambled out of the water and ran to the bank and all the way home.

When he was in dry furs, and Two-Eyes was drying off in a cloud of steam by the fire, Littlenose began to think about the fish in the ice. It must have been there a long time. The winter was more than half-way through. It was several weeks since the Sun Dance. And yet the fish was well preserved. He remembered a journey he had made with a hunting party to the great Ice Cap, and the dead animals he had seen there, frozen into the ice. There was a good idea here somewhere. It only required working out by some clever person . . . like himself. Meanwhile, he would like a closer look at the fish.

Without Two-Eyes this time. The good idea was getting stronger in his mind all the time, and he collected his boy-size stone axe from his own special corner of the cave before he set off back to the river.

He found the frozen perch easily. It was only a few steps from the place where he and Two-Eyes had fallen in. Already the hole was partly frozen over again in the intense cold. Littlenose examined the fish carefully then, kneeling down, he began to chip the ice all round with his axe. He worked slowly, but occasionally, the ice gave a warning creak.

Soon the ice was cut quite through, and the piece with the perch floated on the water underneath. Littlenose got his fingers under the edge and, with a great deal of effort, lifted the ice block, complete with

fish, out of the hole, and laid it on the
surface.

He could see the
perch properly now from
the side. Its bright
colours shone clearly
through the ice.
Carefully lifting
the block of
ice on to
his shoulder,
Littlenose set
off back to the cave. The wonderful idea
was almost completely worked out in his
mind now. But he wouldn't tell anyone
until all the details were complete. With a
sigh of relief, Littlenose put the heavy ice
down on the floor of the cave and studied
it again. The heat from the fire was beginning

to melt the ice and make a puddle on the floor. There was already a puddle where Two-Eyes had dried off, and Mum would go mad at the sight of one puddle, let alone two. So, to save a mess, he lifted the ice and placed it in a large clay bowl which lay near the fire. Then he sat back to think again about his brilliant idea.

It was simple. If a fish could stay fresh like this in a block of ice for more than half the winter, then why couldn't other things, such as deer and woolly rhinoceros? And all the other creatures which the Neanderthal folk hunted for food. Littlenose imagined huge blocks of ice, each containing a large animal ready to be thawed out for cooking and eating during the winter when food was scarce. If the animals were put in a hole in the ground, or even in a special cave, and covered with water, the first frosts of winter would do the rest. "I'll be famous for this, Two-Eyes," he said.

Two-Eyes didn't respond. He was fast asleep in a corner. He reckoned that he had had enough of Littlenose, ice and everything for one day.

Littlenose went to have another look at the lump of ice in the bowl, and found that it had almost all melted away and the fins of the perch were sticking out. Even as he watched, the last piece of ice slid from the perch's body so that it flopped on to its side in the shallow puddle in the bottom of the bowl. Littlenose reached out to touch it . . . and jumped back. The fish moved. It did it again. It flipped its tail, then started wriggling and gasping in the small

drop of water left. It was *alive*!

Quickly, Littlenose fetched the water jar
from Mum's cooking corner and tipped it
into the bowl until it was half full and the
perch, looking a bit surprised at where it
found itself, swam round and round.

Littlenose was entranced. "You can be
my new pet," he said. "I shall call you
Green-fin because you have green fins."
Green-fin looked up at Littlenose, and
Littlenose could have sworn that the little
perch smiled at him. "Come and meet
your new friend," he called to Two-Eyes.

But before Two-Eyes could even waken, there were voices at the entrance to the cave. Mum and Dad, back from visiting a neighbour.

"What are you doing messing about with Mum's cooking pots?" said Dad. He looked into the bowl. "What the–?" he gasped in surprise.

"It's a fish," said Littlenose. "It's– "

"I know what it is," Dad interrupted him. "It's fresh fish. And at this time of year! Delicious!"

Littlenose was horrified. "He's my new pet," he cried.

"Don't talk nonsense," said Dad. "It's fresh fish. Mum! Are there any of those mushrooms left?" He licked his lips and started throwing more wood on the fire.

"He's not for *eating*!" exclaimed Littlenose.

"Of course, he is," said Dad. "Why do you think that fish were put in the river in the first place?" And he picked up a flint knife and tested the edge with his thumb, licking his lips as he did.

This was too much for Littlenose. He brushed Dad to one side, grabbed Green-fin from the bowl and ran like the wind to the river. He ran and slid out across the ice to the hole he had cut with his axe. The water was already freezing over the hole, but Littlenose broke through it with his foot. Then he gently placed the perch in the water. "Goodbye Green-fin," he said. "You'll never know what a lucky escape you had." And with a flick of its tail, the fish vanished into the depths of the river.

Well, that was that, but what could he do now? Littlenose didn't feel like going home at the moment. Then, he remembered his wonderful idea of preserving meat in blocks of ice. All he needed really was a cave, some water and a dead woolly rhinoceros or something similar. The water was no problem. The woolly rhinoceros bit could be tricky, but now was as good a time as any to find a cave. The problem with caves was that they had a tendency to belong to people. And people might be less than understanding about having a dead rhinoceros on top of them, even if it *were* safely frozen into a block of ice.

While he had been thinking, Littlenose had been walking along the river, on the ice. Things looked different from this angle. The high bank, for instance. The river had washed it away so much that you could walk along by the water's edge under it. Worth remembering for wet weather. Why not try it now? Littlenose began to make his way along the edge of the ice, the river bank arching above his head.

And there was a cave!

Completely hidden from above, there was a wide opening in the bank. This could be just what he was looking for. He went inside.

It was fantastic. The floor of the cave was a sheet of ice and the walls glistened with ice also. But, that was not all. Water had dripped through the roof and frozen to form icicles, thousands of them, all shapes and sizes. Some were so long that they reached all the way to the floor. Littlenose walked among the columns of ice. What could all this ice be for? It surely must have some purpose. The river had washed

a lot of driftwood into the cave mouth, and Littlenose picked up a stout stick. How strong was the ice? He hit one of the larger icicles. But it didn't break. Instead it made a loud ringing sound that echoed around the cave. He struck another – and it did the same, but sounding a different note. It was a sort of music. Not Neanderthal music. That consisted of lots of loud hand-clapping and even louder singing. He ran the end of the stick along a row of the smaller icicles, and it was beautiful! A gentle tinkling that hung in the icy air long after he had stopped.

For the rest of the afternoon Littlenose made beautiful music with the stick and the icicles. The music echoed throughout the cave and down the river. It rang across the snowy landscape to the caves of the

Neanderthal folk. They didn't understand. They were even afraid, and looked at one another in wonder. "What is it?" they said. Dad heard it as he sat grumbling about not getting his fresh fish, with mushrooms. "Magic," he said darkly. "No good will come of it. Mark my words!"

Two-Eyes heard the strange music, too. It didn't mean a lot to him. Mammoths tended to be tone-deaf. But they also tended to get lonely, and he decided to look for Littlenose. He followed his trail in the snow away from the caves and along the river bank. He lost the trail there, and walked along the bank, the strange music getting louder with every step he took. The sound seemed to come from somewhere below his feet, and he stood close to the edge and peered over. The edge of the bank crumbled under his weight, and he rolled head over heels in the snow. He landed with a thump at the edge of the ice and the entrance to the cave.

Littlenose was still making music, running here and there, striking first this icicle with his stick, then that. He was so busy that he didn't see Two-Eyes. Two-Eyes saw him first, and ran towards him. But the icy floor of the cave was smooth and slippery and, for the second time that day, Two-Eyes found himself sliding, unable to stop, straight for Littlenose.

Littlenose saw him at the last moment and jumped clear, and Two-Eyes crashed into one of the bigger icicles, bringing it down with a ringing crash. He spun round and hit another and another. Each brought others with it, and the air was filled with a

thousand pieces of falling ice, and a last crescendo of the wonderful music.

Then there was complete silence.

Littlenose was close to tears. "Look what you've done," he said to Two-Eyes. "Now there will be no more music!" Two-Eyes hung his head in shame.

After a moment Littlenose said," Never mind. The icicles would have melted in the spring anyway. There will be more next winter, and we can come back then and make more music. Now, I know. *That's* why the ice is!"

And together they left the cave and made their way back along the bank towards home . . . and supper.

The Ice Monster

When Littlenose was alive, the hills and woods and rivers looked very much as they do today. But the great Ice Cap still covered the northern lands to an enormous depth and sent freezing winds sweeping down throughout the dark winter days. Then, the Neanderthal folk crouched in their caves around blazing fires, and passed the time by telling each other stories. And

some of the best of these stories were about the Ice Cap itself.

"It's a terrible place," the storyteller would say. "Long before you even see it, the air gets colder and colder until it hurts to breathe. The trees get smaller and smaller until they are not higher than your hand."

"And the Ice Cap?" the listeners would ask.

"It is grim and fearful," the storyteller

would continue, "but also strangely beautiful. At daybreak, it is a jagged mass of green and blue shadow; at sunset, it blazes with crimson fire; and in the noon sun, it is so dazzlingly white that a man might go blind from looking at it for more than a short moment. Here is the home of the ice monsters. Few, who have seen them, have lived to tell of it. It is said that they are taller than ten men, with enormous jaws and long scaly tails, and their roaring can be heard for great distances. Their strength is so great that they hurl boulders of ice down on the heads of anyone foolish enough to venture into their lands."

The storyteller would shudder at the horror of the scene he had just described. And his audience would shudder too, enjoying every word.

Littlenose asked Dad about the monsters. "Stuff and nonsense," he snorted.

Then Littlenose asked Uncle Redhead, who was the cleverest person in the whole world. "Monsters? Of course, there are. I've seen them."

"Aren't they dangerous?" asked Littlenose.

"Not them," laughed Uncle Redhead. "They're too old to harm a mouse. There are much more dangerous things to beware of at the Ice Cap than those poor beasts."

Littlenose was very puzzled by his uncle's words. He decided that first thing next morning he would set off for the Ice Cap and see for himself. However, next morning Mum dragged him unwillingly to Old Skinflint the tailor for a new pair of furs. And the day after that he had to go with Dad to collect firewood. And then he forgot all about the Ice Cap.

Now, Littlenose's dad was an expert hunter, and he was determined that Littlenose would be one, too, when he grew up. He had promised that Littlenose could accompany a hunting party some day as part of his education, and now that day had arrived.

Littlenose was overjoyed but mum wasn't so happy. However, when Dad told her it was a horse hunt, she felt better about it. Horses were hunted not for food but for their skins, which were very valuable. Hunting horses meant plodding patiently along behind a herd and waiting for a horse to break a leg, or die, or just get left far behind, when there was a chance it might become an easy prey. It was far from

exciting but it was fairly safe.

Littlenose set off with his dad and the other men early in the morning. They soon found a herd of horses, grazing and wandering slowly in a northerly direction. Keeping carefully down-wind, the hunters followed them . . . for more than a week. A few animals were caught but not enough, and the hunt went on day after weary day. Then they lost the horses.

During the night, the horses doubled back and by morning were miles away. The men were furious. They all blamed each other and ran hither and thither, but the horses were out of sight.

"Now," thought Littlenose, "we'll turn back for home."

But among the hunters was a man by the name of Nosey. He was called Nosey because, even for a Neanderthal man, his nose was exceptionally handsome. And useful. Now he knelt down and sniffed and snuffled among the stones and grass. After a moment, he stood up and pointed north. "That's the way they went," he said.

"Are you sure?" asked the others.

"Quite sure," replied Nosey, so they trudged on.

The weather grew colder and the

country more bare, as the trail took them farther north. They left the trees behind, and were soon travelling over stony ground that was permanently frozen, while an icy wind never stopped blowing. After several days, it was obvious that they had lost all trace of the horses, and that for once Nosey had been wrong. They decided that next morning they would turn back.

But morning brought a very unpleasant surprise. There was a thick white mist and the hunters could barely see. Keeping close to each other, they set off in what they hoped was the right direction.

It was late in the afternoon when Dad help up his hand and said, "Listen." No one could hear a thing, and they started off again.

"Listen, I can hear something," said

Littlenose. And this time, they drew together fearfully, as out of the mist came a distant low growling. It faded away, then became louder and louder, till it was a roar that seemed to fill the air.

"What is it ?" said one man. "If only we could see."

"I don't know," said another. "But at least if we can't see it, it can't see us . . . whatever it is."

"I suggest we stay put," said Dad. "It'll soon be dark and we might as well make camp now."

As they did so, it began to get lighter. The mist was clearing and they were struck dumb by the sight of what lay in front of them. The sun was setting and the sky was red. They found that they had been marching over a flat, bare plain; but a mile or two in front the plain ended abruptly. Flaming and sparkling, like fire, against the darkening sky, was a great mountain-like mass. It reached half-way to the clouds and stretched far out of sight on either hand. As the sun dropped below the horizon, the colour faded to deep blue and green and, finally, to a misty grey as darkness came down. The hunters watched silently and again drew closer to one another, as the terrible growling and roaring filled the air.

They looked at each other. "The Ice Cap," they said.

"The monsters," said Littlenose.

Nobody slept that night. Apart from the cold, the awful sounds filled the darkness.

When daylight came, things looked a little better. The noises from the Ice Cap stopped and, in the sun, its peaks and pinnacles sparkled like a thousand diamonds.

Now that they knew where they were, the hunters could head for home. But first, they would have to find some more food, as their supplies were almost used up. Near the camp, one of them found the tracks of a herd of musk oxen, so, leaving Littlenose in charge, the men set off on the trail.

Littlenose felt quite grown-up. But he soon grew bored. He looked towards the Ice Cap, the main part of which was some way off. However, the nearest of the broken ice hummocks was really quite close. There had been no sound from the ice for a long time. The monsters must be asleep. Surely, going a little closer could do no harm!

Warily, he walked towards the ice. He passed the first pieces and went on,

stopping to listen now and again, and
keeping a careful watch. But the only
sounds were the wind and the steady drip
of water. There was not a single sign of a
monster. Just as he approached the foot of

the Ice Cap proper, he felt a sudden chill.
The sun had disappeared behind a black
cloud. Drops of rain pattered on the ice
and quickly became a downpour.

Littlenose looked about him for shelter, then started running towards a wide opening in the face of the ice. As he reached it, there came a blinding flash of lightning, followed by a peal of thunder, which echoed and crashed, as if it were the end of the world.

In between flashes, Littlenose's shelter was as black as night; but the lightning flared down through the ice so that the cavern glowed like green and blue fire. A sudden gust of wind blew the rain through the entrance, so Littlenose hurried farther in. When the next flash came, he froze with horror.

Towering over him in the flickering light was the most terrible thing he had ever seen. Taller than ten men, with enormous jaws and a long scaly tail, a

fearsome animal was poised ready to spring. Littlenose tried to run but his feet wouldn't move. He just stared, wide-eyed. Then it was dark again and the horror disappeared. He turned to flee . . . then stopped. His only way of escape was back out of the cave, and the monster would be upon him before he had taken two steps. Perhaps, if he stayed absolutely still, it would go away.

He crouched down and didn't make a sound. And neither did the monster! Littlenose could hear the drip of water and the sounds of the storm outside the cave but there was not even the sound of breathing. The monster must have gone.

But if it had, he would surely have heard it move. A huge animal like that was bound to make *some* sound.

Next moment, there came the brightest lightning flash of all.

And not only was the monster still there, but its eyes seemed to dart fire at this small creature, who had invaded its lair.

Littlenose was frantic. He dared not run but he dared not stay.

The thunder began to
die away in the distance
as the storm passed,
and daylight
began to
filter
into
the
cave
as the
dark clouds
rolled away.

"It's bound to see me now," thought Littlenose. But, as the light grew stronger and he strained his eyes to peer into the shadows, he could see nothing! There was no monster. Just a blank wall of ice. Where had it gone? He hadn't been dreaming. He *had* seen it, as tall as ten men, crouched ready to spring; and there wasn't a crack a mouse could have hidden in, let alone something *that* big.

At that moment, the sun came fully out, and Littlenose's heart leaped as the awful creature was suddenly there again . . . but it didn't move, and Littlenose saw why. It was frozen into the ice. Like the small fish he had sometimes seen in the river in winter, the creature was imprisoned and harmless. How many thousands of years it had remained like that, he had no way of knowing, but now he understood Uncle Redhead's words about the ice monsters being too old to harm anyone. Hunters, who had been frightened as he had been, had made up the tales told round the fires. The roaring and growling must simply be pieces of ice breaking and falling from the Ice Cap . . . not being thrown down by anyone or anything.

What a story this was going to make when he got back!

"Goodbye, poor old monster," he said softly, and left the cavern.

He didn't tell his dad or any of the hunting party. He decided to save it till he got home. But when he did try to tell of his adventure, no one would listen. In fact, he was scolded by Dad for having left the camp unguarded.

Only Uncle Redhead believed him, but he, after all, was the cleverest person in the whole world.

Urk

One cold winter's day, Littlenose with Dad
and several of the hunters of the tribe were
making their way through the forest. Snow
lay thick on the ground and only very
feeble light came from the sun, which lay
dull and red just above the horizon.
Suddenly, one of the men pulled down
some long streamers of ivy from the trunk
of a tree. For this was not a hunting

expedition. The men were gathering green foliage to decorate the Sun Dance. The Neanderthal folk believed that the days grew shorter in winter because the sun was weak and tired. So, in the darkest, coldest time of the year, they held a dance for the sun. they thought that if there was no Sun Dance, the sun might go out altogether. But the Sun Dance had never failed them yet.

The ivy was added to a pile of greenery already lying on the ground. "That's about as much as we can carry," said Dad. "We'd better start back." He called Littlenose.

Littlenose, who had wandered off by himself into the trees, didn't answer. Dad called again, impatiently, and Littlenose looked up and beckoned. "There's something funny here," he called.

"Never mind that. Leave it and hurry," cried Dad.

"I think it's a man," called back Littlenose. "Lying in the snow. He might be dead. Come and see."

The hunters hurried to where Littlenose stood pointing at a dark bundle on the ground.

"We'll soon see," said Dad. "Stand back, everybody." And he leaned forward and prodded the object with the handle of his spear. Nothing happened, so he prodded a bit harder, and succeeded in turning whatever it was right over.

It was a man. He didn't appear to be very big but, among the furs, could just be made out an ear and a pair of eyebrows. And from one end, there stuck an unmistakable pair of feet.

One of the hunters bent over. "I wonder who he is? I don't think he's one of our people."

"He couldn't be a Straightnose, could he?" asked another.

Straightnoses were people who lived by following the game herds they hunted. They were very clever and the tribe hated and feared them.

"Not tall enough for a Straightnose," said Dad. "But let's get him home before he does die, then we can worry about who he is."

They made a rough stretcher from animal skins and a pair of spears then, very gently, lifted the stranger onto it, and set off. When the party reached the caves, the Old Man came forward. He stooped down and carefully pulled the furs from the

man's face. He was unlike anyone they had ever seen. He wasn't a Straightnose, but he didn't appear to be a Neanderthal either. His face was broad and flat with a rather straggly beard. His hair was black and hung in a fringe. But most surprising was his nose. It was broad and flat like his face, not large and snuffly like those looking down at him.

"Where has he come from?" they all asked.

"He's half-frozen and probably half-starved as well," said the Old Man. "I suggest that we get him into the warm until he recovers, then he will have to be fed. Who will take into their cave?"

No one moved. Rescuing travellers lost in the forest was one thing. Provided in them with board and lodging was quite another.

Then Littlenose spoke up. "I found him," he said. "I'll look after him. Won't we?" and he looked round at Dad.

Dad said, "Well, er . . . "

But Mum pushed through the crowd. "Of course, we will," she said. The rest of the tribe, looking rather relieved, disappeared into their caves.

For the rest of the day, Littlenose sat by his patient, while Mum piled logs onto the fire until a glow began to return to the little man's cheeks.

It was evening when, suddenly, Littlenose jumped up. "He's moving," he cried. "Look!"

Slowly, the stranger opened his eyes and tried to sit up. Littlenose hurried to help him. He looked confused, and obviously wondered how he came to be in a strange cave. Littlenose said, "Are you feeling better, sir? You've had a long sleep." But the only reply was a puzzled look.

Then Mum tried. "You must be hungry. Would you like something to eat?"

The stranger held his head on one side and frowned, but still said nothing.

Now, Dad joined in. "Let's start at the beginning," he said. Speaking slowly and loudly, and pointing at each of them in

turn, he said, "Me . . . Dad. Her . . . Mum.
Him . . . Littlenose . . . You?" pointing at
the stranger.

The little man frowned again and said
something that sounded like, "Urk!"

"That's it," said Dad, "his name's Urk!
Once he gets the hang of our language, he
can tell us about himself. I just don't know
what you would do without me."

Mum filled a clay bowl with pieces of boiled rhinoceros. "Here you are, Urk," she said. "You must be hungry."

Again, Urk looked puzzled but, when he saw the bowl and what was in it, his face was split by an enormous grin. He took the bowl and, before Mum had turned away, he handed it back . . . empty! He nodded vigorously and pointed at the bowl.

"Gracious, he wants more!" cried Mum, and gave him another helping. That vanished as quickly as the first. Then Urk wiped his mouth with his hand, lay down, and went back to sleep.

"Well, there doesn't seem to be much wrong with *him*," said Dad. "Do you think he plans to stay for long?" Whether planned or not, Urk was in no hurry to leave. For one thing, despite all his eating, he was very weak and could barely hobble from his sleeping corner to the fire and back.

But as his strength returned, his appetite grew. He had usually finished his meal and was looking for more, while Littlenose and his parents were still at the first course. In the end, they took to having an enormous breakfast before Urk woke in the morning. Then there was a better chance of lasting throughout the day without starving.

Eventually, Urk and Littlenose came to understand each other quite well. By signs, odd noises and pictures scratched on the floor of the cave, Littlenose gradually learned how Urk came to be found exhausted, frozen and starving in the forest. One night, after a very meagre supper (for everyone but Urk that is) Littlenose told Urk's story to his parents. "I don't think his name is Urk anyway," he said. "All his words sound like that." Dad didn't look too pleased at this. "He belongs to a tribe that lives four weeks' march north of here."

"But that would mean that they live beyond the Ice Cap," interrupted Dad.

"They live at the foot of the Ice Cap," continued Littlenose. "By the seashore. It's always winter there, and it's dark for weeks and weeks on end. They hunt for food as we do but the animals are different. Most of them are white. The people never have fruit or honey although they have lots of fish. There are bears and foxes and wolves and deer but the animals, which live in the sea, are fat and good to eat, although very difficult to catch. They have sleek fur and great tusks like a mammoth. The biggest things they hunt are the fish. Some are fifty paces long! One of them can feed the whole tribe right through the winter. The sea is often frozen, and the hunters can walk far out from the land to spear the fish. It's very dangerous and many of them get drowned or eaten. Urk was one of a party out on the ice after some big fish. One attacked them and broke the ice, and the piece that Urk was on drifted away. It had almost melted away to nothing when he managed to get ashore near the mouth of the river. He followed the river hoping to find people. But we found him first."

Dad said nothing when Littlenose had finished.

But Mum said, "What an adventure! He must be very brave."

"Don't be ridiculous," snorted Dad. "That's nothing but a pack of lies! Making up wild tales to amuse Littlenose is one thing. Expecting us to believe them is another."

"He drew me a picture, too," said Littlenose, holding out a flat piece of bone. Scratched into its surface was the outline

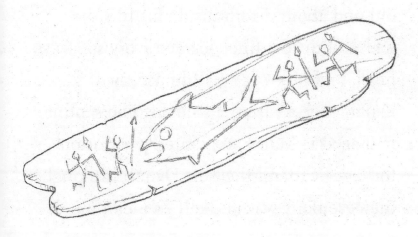

of a fish with tiny figures surrounding it with spears.

"Funny stories and now comic pictures," roared Dad. "We must be the only Neanderthal tribe with a resident comedian!" And, laughing at his own joke, he walked out of the cave.

Littlenose didn't laugh, though. He made a hole in Urk's piece of bone and threaded it on a piece of sinew to wear round his neck.

By the day of the Sun Dance, Urk was out and about. From inside his furs, he had produced a finely-carved ivory spear head, and now occupied himself with making a shaft from a straight pine sapling.

The Old Man had granted permission for Urk to attend the Sun Dance, although the ceremony wasn't likely to mean much to him. However, Littlenose managed to explain that there would be feasting, and Urk was very enthusiastic.

So was Dad. "It'll be the first square meal we've had in days," he grumbled.

"Don't be so mean," said Mum. "This is the season of goodwill."

But everyone was in a very cheerful frame of mind by the time Dad, Mum and Littlenose set off with Urk. Urk's sleek furs were very fine, and he carried his spear.

The decorated trees sparkled in the light of the bonfires and torches. The food was more plentiful and delicious than ever before. This was Littlenose's favourite part of the Sun Dance and Urk positively revelled in it. The tribe watched him and laughingly called him the new Neanderthal Eating Champion.

After the feasting, came the dancing. A space was cleared and the hunters performed dances, which told of great deeds of the past. Some pretended to be bears and others mammoths. For music, everyone sang and clapped their hands until the snow shook from the trees with the joyful sounds.

At last, the dancers stopped, exhausted, and everyone applauded them. The Old Man was about to make a closing speech when a commotion broke out.

It was Urk. He was trotting round and round in circles waving his spear, and the crowd was backing away nervously. The people moved back until Urk had cleared a wide space in front of the main bonfire. Now he stood leaning on his spear, looking at them. Was he going to attack them? But he started to sing, softly at first, then more loudly, clapping his hands in time to the tune. Then he danced. The people began to clap with him as he hopped and skipped

in a strange pattern, dragging his spear behind him, with the point dug deep into the sandy ground. He danced almost to one

edge of the clearing, then swung back to
the other. It was very entertaining but what
was it all about?

It was Littlenose who first spotted what
Urk was doing. Littlenose, afraid that he
would be trampled underfoot, had climbed
into the low branches of a tree. Looking

down, he saw that Urk was drawing a picture on the ground. It was the same as his carving. Urk was drawing an enormous fish! Now Urk paused. He stood to one edge of the circle and started to sing again. But this time the song was different. No one could understand the words but, as he sang, he danced, and an exciting story unfolded before them.

The story told of Urk and his tribe, hungry and weak. Urk came out of his cave and scanned the sea. But there was nothing. Seven times he peered over the imaginary waves and seven times he returned to his starving family. On the eighth time, he peered under his hand and started to turn away yet again. Then he stopped and looked back out to sea. He wasn't sure. Had he seen something. He strained his eyes and held his breath. His audience held theirs, too. The suspense was terrible. But it was a fish! To the great relief of everyone, Urk set off in pursuit across the ice. The excitement of the story had the audience on tiptoe. They cheered as Urk hurled his spear at the fish drawn on the ground. They gasped as he leapt onto its back. They groaned as it threw him off into the water. Time and again it seemed he would lose the fish but now it was growing weaker until, with a cry of triumph, Urk plunged his spear deep into the fish's heart. There was a moment of silence then thunderous applause.

Urk was carried home shoulder high after the Sun Dance, and the moon was setting when the last of the tribe dropped wearily but happily into bed.

It was late when people began to appear
the day after the Sun Dance. Urk slept
almost until nightfall then woke in time to
eat one of his customary gigantic meals.
But he seemed preoccupied. He fussed
around with his spear and was very irritable
when Littlenose went to sit beside him.

In the night, Littlenose woke and saw
the shadowy figure of Urk disappearing
into the darkness. Pulling on a fur robe,
Littlenose crept after him. From the
shadow of the trees, Littlenose watched as
Urk searched about on the ground. In the
faint moonlight, he saw him pick up two
forked branches and stick them in the
ground, like pot supports at a cooking fire.
Then he laid his ivory-tipped spear across
the forks. It pointed north.

As the moon came fully out from behind

the clouds, Urk began to dance. Slowly, he paced around the spear, his arms held out to the moon, while he sang a song so sad that the tears ran down Littlenose's cheeks. He still couldn't understand Urk's language but he knew that the song was about being far from home in a strange land.

Feeling that he would never see Urk again, Littlenose returned to the cave, where he curled up in his own special corner and cried himself to sleep.

In the morning, sure enough, Urk was gone. He had taken the meat which Mum had intended having for supper, but had left in its place a beautifully-carved bone picture showing Dad, Mum Littlenose and Two-Eyes in their cave.

The Giant Snowball

Littlenose, like all boys, loved the snow, and in the days when he lived, there was usually snow to be found somewhere at all times of the year. Two-Eyes was not so fond of it. He would join Littlenose in sliding sometimes, but he objected to the way in which the snow caught in his fur and formed into icicles. Then, when he went home, Mum would be angry as the

ice melted and dripped water all over the
floor.

One cold winter's day, the snow lay thick
and smooth over the land. Littlenose,
bundled up in his winter furs, was playing
one of his favourite games. He was following
tracks in the snow. This could be dangerous,

because Littlenose sometimes made mistakes and had once followed what he thought was a red deer, only to find himself suddenly face to face with a sabre-toothed tiger!

Today, he was following what he hoped was a moose, and as usual Two-Eyes was walking behind, pausing from time to time to shake the snow from his coat, and give disgusted little snorts through his trunk.

The tracks were clear, and led through woods, over frozen marshland and up a long hill. Here, however, he lost them. The top of the hill was bare and rocky, and the snow had drifted clear. There was just no way of telling which way the moose had gone.

With a sigh of relief, Two-Eyes shook himself once more, then began to clean his fur with his trunk. Having done this, he found a sheltered spot behind a rock, and settled down for a quiet snooze.

Littlenose, meanwhile, was doing some exploring. Down the hill a little way there was a wood, and he thought there might be something interesting to see there.

But it was just an ordinary wood. Then he found a dead tree. It had been struck by lightning and stood bare and broken. The bark had come off in great pieces and, as Littlenose looked, he had a wonderful idea. There was one piece of bark which was longer than Littlenose himself, and quite broad. It wasn't very heavy, and he was able to drag it across the ground. He pulled it out from under the trees and onto the snowy hillside.

Very carefully, he sat down on the piece

of bark, and nothing happened. He pushed
again, and it moved a little further. With
all his might, Littlenose leaned back and
heaved. The bark shot forward and next
moment he was careering down the hill.

Littlenose clung hard. He had no idea
how to steer, but he laughed and shouted
as his sledge bounced over the snow.

At last, with a thump, he hit a grassy tussock, and went somersaulting through the air. He landed in a deep drift, and scrambled to his feet, brushing the snow out of his hair.

He was amazed to find how far he had travelled. The wood, and the rock where he had left Two-Eyes, seemed very far away.

It was growing late, and Littlenose knew he ought to start for home, but he wanted just one more ride on his sledge. He looked up at the opposite slope. "If I start from up *there*," he thought, "I'll not only go faster because it's steeper, but may be a good way up towards the wood if I'm lucky," and he began to drag the piece of bark over the snow.

He was quite out of breath when he reached the top, and stopped for a moment to get his wind back.

Suddenly, he heard something. He wasn't sure what. Perhaps it was only the wind. He heard it again, but louder, and shivered with fright as he realized what it was.

A wolf!

Almost immediately, a whole pack appeared. With one accord, they threw back their heads and howled, and came trotting across the snow.

Littlenose was terrified. He looked wildly around him for Two-Eyes, but he was far away, up on the opposite hill, beyond the wood.

In a panic, Littlenose turned and threw himself full-length on his piece of bark. It shot forward, and next moment he was hurtling down the hill with the wolf pack in pursuit.

The snow blew up his nose and down his neck, but he didn't care. He lay flat, clinging on for all he was worth, while he bumped and rocked over the hummocky snow.

He glanced back over his shoulder.

The wolves were streaming down the hill, ears back and long red tongues hanging out. Occasionally, one would give a blood-curdling howl, and take an enormous leap forward.

However, the snow was deep for running, and Littlenose drew slowly ahead. He was almost at the foot of the hill now, and he wondered how far up the opposite side his speed would carry him. He wondered if Two-Eyes would see him from beyond the wood. He cranes his neck and tried to see the little mammoth, and was so busy doing this that he didn't see a large rock straight ahead.

The sledge hit the rock with a crash, throwing Littlenose head over heels, and splintering into a thousand pieces of bark.

Littlenose, unhurt, rolled over and over. The wolves, with joyful howls, ran even faster at the thought of a boy for supper.

Littlenose scrambled up. The wolves
were almost on him, and he was a long
way from the top. He began running
towards an enormous fallen pine tree.
With the pack at his heels, he snatched up
a thick tree branch and pulled himself up
on to the roots of the fallen tree.

He was not a moment too soon.

The leading wolf sprang up with snapping
jaws, and Littlenose brought the branch
down hard on its nose. Yelping, it dropped
back, but another came, and then another,
until Littlenose was slashing and swiping
as hard as he could.

He swung his branch once more, and
was almost dragged down as a wolf seized it
in his jaws and snatched it from him.

Now he had nothing.

But there was a lot of snow lying on the

tree-trunk, and Littlenose quickly made a snowball and threw it hard. It caught a wolf in the open jaws, sending it coughing and choking away.

He threw more and more snowballs until he had almost used up all the snow.

Then the wolves drew back. Most of them had sore heads or bloody noses, and they held a council of war to decide what should be done next.

High on the hill, Two-Eyes had wakened from his nap. His fur was dry, and he felt rather hungry. It must be time to go home. He looked around him for Littlenose.

Then he heard the commotion from the foot of the hill. He couldn't see, but it sounded as if Littlenose was up to something. Having got his fur clean, he wasn't very anxious to venture on to the snowy hillside, but he carefully picked his way down to the wood.

The noise was much further on, and Two-Eyes pushed his way through the trees. The moment he saw Littlenose surrounded by the wolves, he forgot all about the snow and his fur.

He put down his head and *charged*!

But he had only taken a few paces before he realized that the slope was steeper than he had thought. He was running much too fast and, before he could stop himself, he lost his footing and tumbled over and over.

Meanwhile, the wolves had decided to have one more attempt at catching Littlenose. The leader gave a howl, and the wolf pack leapt forward. They were met by Littlenose's few remaining snowballs, and were almost upon him when suddenly they stopped.

They were all looking up the hill,
although Littlenose couldn't see anything
for the branches of the tree. Then one wolf
gave a yelp and turned and ran with its tail
between its legs. The rest followed, and
Littlenose saw why. An enormous snowball
was bounding down the hill! Littlenose had

never seen anything like it, and neither had the wolves. They fled madly before it, but not before several had been bowled over and sent flying through the air.

The snowball hurtled on, and the wolves, scrambling over each other in panic, dashed madly away until their howling died in the distance. The snowball rolled a few more metres, then hit a birch sapling and burst apart in a great shower of snow.

Sitting in the middle was Two-Eyes.

"Two-Eyes," shouted Littlenose, "how clever of you! You arrived just in time."

But Two-Eyes wasn't feeling particularly clever. He was so dizzy he could hardly stand. Littlenose took his trunk in his hand and, with Two-Eyes leaving a very wiggly line of footprints in the snow, they set off for home.

100,000 YEARS AGO people wore no clothes. They lived in caves and hunted animals for food. They were called NEANDERTHAL.

50,000 YEARS AGO when Littlenose lived, clothes were made out of fur. But now there were other people. Littlenose called them Straightnoses. Their proper name is HOMO SAPIENS.

5,000 YEARS AGO there were no Neanderthal people left. People wore cloth as well as fur. They built in wood and stone. They grew crops and kept cattle.

1,000 YEARS AGO towns were built, and men began to travel far from home by land and sea to explore the world.

500 YEARS AGO towns became larger, as did the ships in which men travelled. The houses they built were very like those we see today.

100 YEARS AGO people used machines to do a lot of the harder work. They could now travel by steam train. Towns and cities became very big, with factories as well as houses

TODAY we don't hunt for our food, but buy it in shops. We travel by car and aeroplane. Littlenose would not understand any of this. Would YOU like to live as Littlenose did?